ISABEL AND THE HUNGRY COYOTE

Isabel y el coyote hambriento

Written by / Escrito por Keith Polette

Illustrated by / Ilustrado por Esther Szegedy

To my family
—Keith

To Alain, who's always there.
—Esther

Polette, Keith.

　　Isabel and the hungry coyote / written by Keith Polette ; illustrated by
　　Esther Szegedy = Isabel y el coyote hambriento / escrito por Keith Polette ;
　　ilustrado por Esther Szegedy. -- 1st ed. -- Green Bay, WI : Raven Tree
　　Press, 2004, c2003.

　　　　p. cm.

　　　　Audience: grades K-3.
　　　　Text in English with intermittent Spanish words.
　　　　Summary: Retelling of the classic: Little Red Riding Hood.
　　　　ISBN: 0-9724973-0-7

　　　　1. Self-reliance--Juvenile fiction. 2. Coyote--Juvenile fiction. 3. Fairy
　　tales. 4. Bilingual books. I. Szegedy, Esther. II. Title. III. Isabel y el
　　coyote hambriento.

PZ7 .P554 2004　　　　　　　　　　　　2003092182

[E]--dc21　　　　　　　　　　　　　　0406

Printed in the U.S.A.

1 0 9 8 7 6 5 4 3

first edition

ISABEL AND THE HUNGRY COYOTE

Isabel y el coyote hambriento

Written by / Escrito por Keith Polette

Illustrated by / Ilustrado por Esther Szegedy

Raven Tree Press llc

Coyote's stomach rumbled as he prowled the desert for something to eat.

At the mouth of a small, dry valley, he stopped. His yellow eyes flashed as he spotted a girl in a red hood. She was holding a basket and picking desert flowers.

Coyote licked his lips. He crept towards the girl in the caperuza roja.

Picking flores, the girl in the red hood sang softly.

With his eyes narrowed into slits, Coyote crept closer. And closer. The girl in the caperuza roja picked more flores.

As Coyote drew near, he prepared to pounce. But suddenly, his stomach rumbled! It churned and gurgled and grumbled!

The girl whirled around. "Señor Coyote!" said the girl, "What do you want?"

"Ay," said Coyote, as his stomach rumbled, "I wanted to say, ah, good morning."

"Buenos dias to you," said the girl as she took a step back, "My name is Isabel."

"My, that is a pretty red hood you are wearing Isabel," said Coyote.

His yellow eyes flashed. He inched closer to her.

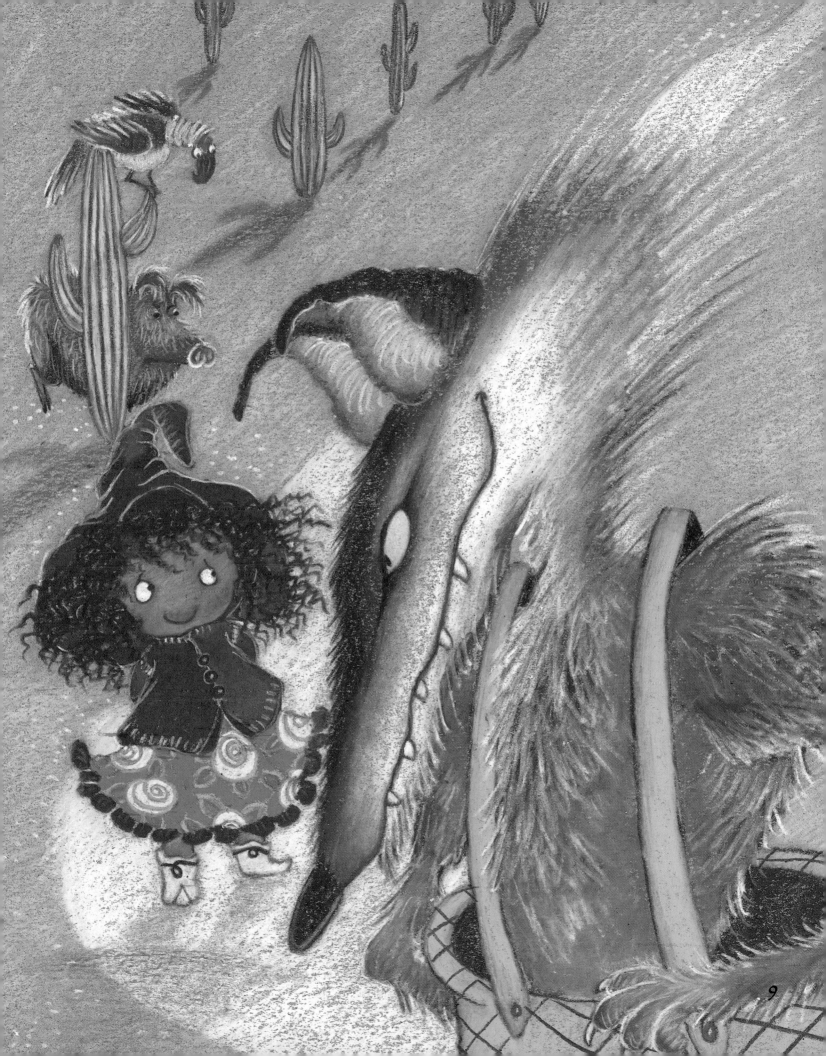

9

"Gracias, Señor, thank you, sir. This caperuza roja keeps the sun from my face," said Isabel as she took another step back.

"I see," said Coyote, "And where are you going?"

Licking his lips, he inched closer.

"I am going to visit my grandmother," said Isabel taking another step back.

"Oh? And where does your abuela live?" asked Coyote.

"She lives at the end of this arroyo," said Isabel, "Look, there is her casa."

Isabel pointed to the adobe house at the end of the small desert valley.

Coyote's yellow eyes flashed. He looked at the adobe casa and then at Isabel. He thought to himself, "This girl in the caperuza roja would make a fine lunch! Ah, but if I wait, I may have both her and her abuela for my comida!"

Coyote sniffed the air and said, "What do you have in the basket?"

"Spicy tamales and red chile sauce," said Isabel, "Would you like one?"

"Oh, no!" said Coyote, "I never eat tamales and chile sauce! They are like fire, like fuego. They burn my mouth!" snapped Coyote.

Coyote looked to the casa of Isabel's abuela. He said, "I must be going. Goodbye."

"Adiós, Señor," replied Isabel.

Coyote kicked up a little dust. His yellow eyes flashed as he disappeared into the arroyo that led to the casa of Isabel's abuela.

17

When Coyote arrived at the abuela's casa, he found the door open. Licking his lips, he crept inside. The casa was silent and still.

Coyote looked into each room. But he did not see Isabel's abuela.

Just then, he heard Isabel lift the latch of the gate outside. Coyote scampered into the abuela's bedroom. He put on the abuela's nightgown. He jumped into the abuela's bed and pulled the covers up to his chin.

When Isabel arrived, she called, "Hola, Abuela. Are you home?"

Coyote answered, "Sí, sí. Come in Isabel."

Isabel stepped into the casa and went straight to her abuela's bedroom. Coyote said, "I am happy to see you, my dear. Come closer."

Isabel approached the bed. Then she stopped and said, "Why Abuela, what big eyes you have!"

"Oh, my ojos are grandes so I can see you, my dear," said Coyote.

Isabel said, "Why, Abuela, what big ears you have!"

"Oh, my orejas are grandes so I can hear you, m'ija," said Coyote.

Isabel said, "Why Abuela, what big arms you have!"

"Oh, my brazos are grandes so I can hug you, m'ija," said Coyote.

Isabel said, "Why Abuela, what a big, big mouth you have!"

"Ah, my boca is muy grande so I can eat you, m'ija!" snarled Coyote.

Growling a terrible growl, Coyote leapt from the bed. His yellow eyes flashed as he grabbed Isabel with his powerful brazos. He opened his big boca to swallow her.

Isabel trembled as she looked into Coyote's wide mouth. She squirmed to get free, but Coyote's arms were very strong; they were muy fuerte!

Isabel said, "That was Coyote. He wanted me for his comida, but I flung a basket of tamales and chile sauce into his boca grande!"

"You are a brave and clever girl!" said Isabel's abuela.

"But Abuela," said Isabel, "I brought those tamales and chile sauce for you."

"Do not worry, m'ija," said her abuela, "We can make more."

Which is exactly what they did.

Vocabulario / Vocabulary

Spanish	English
flores	flowers
el señor	sir
buenos dias	good morning
gracias	thank you
la caperuza	hood
roja	red
la abuela	grandmother
el arroyo	a small desert valley
la casa	house
la comida	lunch
el fuego	fire
adiós	goodbye
hola	hello
si	yes
los ojos	eyes
grandes	big
las orejas	ears
mija	my dear
los brazos	arms
la boca	mouth
muy grande	very big
la siesta	nap
ay	oh
boca grande	big mouth
muy fuerte	very strong